MORE GREAT GRAPHIC NOVEL SERIES AVAILABLE FROM PAPERCUTZ

BARBIE #1

BARBIE PUPPY PARTY

ANNE OF GREEN BAGELS #1

DISNEY FAIRIES #18

FUZZY BASEBALL

THE GARFIELD SHOW #6

THE LUNCH WITCH #1

MINNIE & DAISY #1

NANCY DREW DIARIES #7

THE RED SHOES

SCARLETT

THE SISTERS #1

THE SMURFS #21

THEA STILTON #6

TROLLS #1

THE SECRET
OF THE GEMS

PAPERCUTZ™

NEW YORK

BARBIE STAR LIGHT ADVENTURE "The Secret of the Gems"
Tini Howard – Writer
Jules Rivera – Artist
Matt Herms – Colorist (cover)
Matteo Baldrighi and Jules Rivera – Colorists
Cardinal Rae – Letterer

Dawn Guzzo – Design/Production
Sasha Kimiatek – Production Coordinator
Bethany Bryan – Editor
Jeff Whitman – Assistant Managing Editor
Jim Salicrup
Editor-in-Chief

ISBN: 978-1-62991-610-1 paperback edition
ISBN: 978-1-62991-611-8 hardcover edition

Papercutz books may be purchased for business or promotional use.
For information on bulk purchases please contact Macmillan Corporate
and Premium Sales Department at (800) 221-7945 x5442.

Printed in Canada
December 2016 by Marquis

Distributed by Macmillan
First Printing

5

6

"JUST WAIT TILL YOU TRY DAD'S COOKING."

WHEN WE'RE ALL DONE EATING...

...WE'LL BE FULLER THAN THE MOON!

WELCOME HOME, PRINCESS.

I *MISSED* THIS!

WE MISSED YOU, TOO, BARBIE. I CAN'T WAIT TO HEAR ABOUT ALL OF YOUR ADVENTURES.

NOW THAT WE'RE ALL ON THE GROUND, REMIND ME OF EVERYONE'S NAMES?

YEP! DAD, YOU REMEMBER...

"SAL-LEE, A HOVERBOARD RACING *LEGEND*...

HI THERE!

"SHEENA AND KAREENA, WHO ARE GRAVITY *GENIUSES*...

PLEASED TO--

--MEET YOU!

"AND LEO, BOTH PRINCE AND PILOT!"

CHARME

GALACTIMANGO PUNCH *FLOATS*, FIREFLY PIE, AAAAND NACHOS!

DIG IN!

ER, DAD...

WE WERE ALL *REALLY* EXCITED TO EXPLORE PARA-DEN. MAYBE...WE COULD MAKE IT A PICNIC?

THAT'S A *GREAT* IDEA! I JUST GOT A NEW BLANKET! FOOD'S BETTER OUT IN NATURE!

⇟*PHEW!*⇞ I WAS GONNA HAVE TO HOVERBOARD IN THE HALL IF I DIDN'T GET OUTSIDE SOON. SHIPS MAKE ME STIR-CRAZY!

--SEE!?

WHAT HAPPENED TO THE FOREST?

THE FOG HAS BEEN SO BAD, I COULDN'T SEE A THING! I CAME HERE ON MY WALK JUST LAST WEEK! I DIDN'T SEE ANYTHING.

HEY, AREN'T THERE SUPPOSED TO BE TREES HERE?

VROOOM

BEEP BEEP

CRASH

I GREW UP IN THIS FOREST. I RODE MY FIRST HOVERBOARD HERE!

I GOTTA STOP THIS.

HEY!

SSHINK

COOL, IT WORKED! WE'LL BRING 'EM BACK, OKAY!?

WE'RE DOING ALL WE CAN TO STOP STELLAR INDUSTRIES, BUT...

RRRRRUUMMMMM

VRRROOOOOMM

STOOOOOOOOOP!

"...SHE JUST MOVED IN!"

I *WILL* THEN!

NO ONE TAKES AWAY THE HOMES OF MY FRIENDS--

DON'T WORRY, GUYS. WE'LL GET THIS ALL SORTED OUT!

--ANIMAL OR OTHERWISE!

YOU MUST BE BARBIE!

HELLO, ELLA. THE CONSTRUCTION WORKERS MUST HAVE TOLD YOU I WAS COMING...?

THEY SAID YOU HAD A PROBLEM WITH WHAT WAS GOING ON IN THE FOREST?

WE ALL DID, MS. STELLAR.

I CAN'T UNDERSTAND WHY SOMEONE WOULD MOVE TO PARA-DEN, JUST TO CUT DOWN OUR BEAUTIFUL TREES AND DIG UP OUR GROUND!

I SEE. COME WITH ME, BARBIE. PERHAPS I CAN EXPLAIN.

VOILÀ, BARBIE! INTRODUCING MY *STELLARSHIP!* FEATURING STELLAR TRAVEL, POWERED ONLY BY *PARA-GEMS!*

PARA-GEMS? IS *THAT* WHAT YOU'RE DIGGING FOR OUT THERE?

PARA-GEMS ARE ONE OF THE GALAXY'S FASTEST FUELS! WITH *PARA-GEMS,* MY NEW STELLARSHIP BUSINESS CAN BRING THOUSANDS OF TOURISTS TO PARA-DEN IN THE BLINK OF AN EYE!

FIG II

IT'LL PUT THIS QUAINT, QUIET LITTLE PLANET ON THE GALACTIC TOURISM MAP!

BUT...THE FOREST! SOME OF US LIVE THERE!

BARBIE TRIES TO CALM THE ANIMALS...

STAY CALM, PLEASE!

...BUT IT DOESN'T GO SO WELL.

YOU HEARD HER, EVERYONE. SINGLE FILE!

I'M NOT SURE THIS IS WORKING, BARBIE!

HEY, YOU! CALM DOWN!

SHEENA AND KAREENA TRY TO PROTECT SOME OF THE SMALLER, MORE HELPLESS ANIMALS.

WHERE DID THOSE--

--CHAMELEONS GO?

THERE!

COME BACK HERE!

BARBIE? I THINK--

--WE GOT 'EM!

꒰PHEW!꒱

THIS IS EXACTLY WHAT I MEAN!

I DON'T KNOW, BARBIE--

--WE'RE HAVING FUN!

BOING BOING BOING

THIS IS FUN FOR NOW, BUT THESE ANIMALS NEED A HOME.

WHOA!

I'M NOT SURE OUR BACK YARD MAKES A GOOD HOME FOR ALL THESE ANIMALS.

AND ELLA STELLAR'S PROJECT IS JUST GOING TO KEEP EXPANDING.

I'M SO PROUD OF YOU. BUT I DON'T KNOW THAT YOU'VE THOUGHT THIS ALL THE WAY THROUGH.

MAYBE I HAVEN'T.

HEY, BARBIE? I HAVE A QUESTION.

YEAH, SAL-LEE?

33

OKAY, EVERYONE...

WELCOME HOME!

THIS ISN'T RIGHT. THIS ISN'T ANY KIND OF HOME FOR AN ANIMAL. THEY CAN'T LIVE IN CRANES AND BULLDOZERS!

WELL, WE THOUGHT THAT BY SLOWING THINGS DOWN WE HAVE TIME TO DISCUSS A SOLUTION...

BESIDES, BARBIE IS SAVING PARA-DEN!

FROM *YOUR* EVIL PLAN TO STEAL ALL OF THE PARA-GEMS!

STEAL?!

WHUMP

NO!

≷AACKK!≷

I HAVEN'T STOLEN *ANYTHING!* THIS LAND WAS BOUGHT AND PAID FOR!

THE COUNCIL OF PARA-DEN WAS HAPPY TO SELL ME THIS LAND, BARBIE. THEY LIKE WHAT I'M DOING FOR YOUR PLANET!

BEE-EEEP

MESSAGE FOR YOU, BARBIE. FROM THE HIGH COUNCIL OF PARA-DEN.

OH, NO...

43

BOOM

BOOM

BOOM

NO!

MY PARA-GEMS...

ONE MORE SECOND!

CREEEAAK

SEE? THEY'RE NOT STONES, THEY'RE SEEDS!

⸮GASP⸮

I COMPLETELY UNDERSTAND NOW. I'M SORRY WE WEREN'T HONEST WITH YOUR COUNCIL ABOUT WHAT WE PLANNED TO DO WITH THE PARA-GEMS. I SUPPOSE WE'RE NOT WELCOME HERE ANYMORE?

ON THE CONTRARY! THE COUNCIL AGREES THAT PARA-DEN CAN BE A GREAT TOURIST DESTINATION!

YEAH! HOVERBOARD RACES THROUGH THE WOODS...

AND SURFING--

--ON THE WAVES!

AND EXOTIC WILDLIFE!

ALL THINGS THAT REQUIRE THE PRESERVATION OF OUR AMAZING ECOSYSTEM!

ALL RIGHT, I GET IT. WE CHANGE OUR OPERATIONS FROM MINING TO...FARMING THESE THINGS?

THAT'S RIGHT! BE PATIENT, AND LOVE THE LAND, AND YOU'LL STILL BE ABLE TO USE SOME OF THE PARA-GEMS TO POWER YOUR SHIPS. AND WE CAN'T WAIT TO SEE EVERYONE WHO COMES TO VISIT!

HECK, BARBIE'S DAD WILL PROBABLY COOK FOR THEM!

WELL, YOUNG MAN, THAT'S A NICE THOUGHT, BUT THE STELLARSHIPS HOLD 500 PASSENGERS EACH...

OH...

...WE KNOW...

GEMBERRY DUMPLINGS! ON A STICK, OR SERVED ALONGSIDE OUR HAND-CHURNED FROZEN YOGURT! THEY'RE--WHAT IS IT, BARBIE?

...OUT OF THIS WORLD, DAD!

GROOOAAAN

OH! UM... ARE YOU HERE TO GET SOME DUMPLINGS?

I SURE AM! KEEPING THESE PARA-GEM TREES HAPPY IS HUNGRY WORK!

THE END.

WATCH OUT FOR PAPERCUTZ™

Welcome to the fantasy-filled BARBIE STAR LIGHT ADVENTURE "The Secret of the Gems" graphic novel, by the fabulously futuristic team of Tini Howard, writer, and Jules Rivera, artist. We're thrilled that you're travelled to the farthest reaches of the galaxy to join Barbie on her latest exciting adventure.

If this is your first BARBIE graphic novel, you're in luck because there're two more BARBIE graphic novels also available that we're sure you'll just love!

The first graphic novel is BARBIE "Fashion Superstar." Barbie dreams of a career in fashion, and she just got her first big break—assisting world-famous fashion designer Whitney Yang at her big Spring Fashion Show! But when things start going wrong, it's up to Barbie and her friends to work some fashion miracles. Take a look at the preview starting on the very next page, to experience just a taste of this exciting graphic novel by Sarah Kuhn, writer, and Alitha Martinez, artist.

The second graphic novel is BARBIE PUPPY PARTY. Not only does it star Barbie, it also features Barbie's sisters, Chelsea, Stacie, and Skipper, along with their pet puppies, Honey, Rookie, Taffy, and DJ! The perplexed pooches suspect that the girls have forgotten about their birthday party when they see all the elaborate preparations going on for a party to adopt home-less pets. Can that possibly be the case? The answer awaits in BARBIE PUPPY PARTY!

But if you're a super-Barbie fan and already have these other two graphic novels, and you're looking for more fun graphic novels to enjoy while you're waiting for the next BARBIE novel to appear, may we suggest going to www.papercutz.com to check out some of the other great graphic novels we publish?

So, if you love BARBIE—either on Earth working as a fashion designer or with her sisters and puppies, or in outer space —or just fun, entertaining graphic novels with really cool characters—Papercutz has what you're looking for!

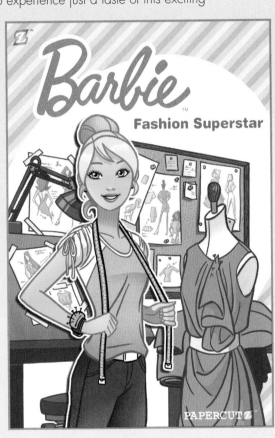

STAY IN TOUCH!

EMAIL: salicrup@papercutz.com
WEB: papercutz.com
TWITTER: @papercutzgn
FACEBOOK: PAPERCUTZGRAPHICNOVELS
FANMAIL: Papercutz, 160 Broadway, Suite 700 East Wing, New York, NY 10038

Don't Miss BARBIE #1 "Fashion Superstar" available now!